# Carlie Rae and Crew First Day of School

Written By: Letia Wyatt
Illustrated By: Fauzia Najm

Carlie Rae always knew that she was a special little girl. Mama would tell her how beautiful and smart she was. So it just stuck with her.

She had such an adventurous kind of mind. One that took her to mystical and magical places whenever she closed her eyes. Her mama told her that's called having an "imagination."

Carlie's bright smile and imagination were the things she liked best about herself. Soon she would have a chance to learn and explore even more once she began her first day of Kindergarten.

The next day Carlie woke up with a huge smile on her face! "Mama, Mama!" she screamed.

"Yes, Carlie Rae. What is it?".

"Mama it's the first day of school and I get to wear my pretty blue dress with the big yellow flower on it!"

Carlie Rae loved Yellow! She thought that it shined bright like the sun and made her feel warm and fuzzy inside.

"Yep! It is!" her Mama said. Are you excited?"
"Yes Ma'am I am!" Carlie Rae said with an
even wider grin.

Today Carlie Rae was really excited to go to school. She had met Mrs. Tenney her new teacher, when her and Mama went to visit the school a few weeks ago.
She had promised the class lots of fun, games and reading!
This was sure to be the best first day of school ever!

Mrs. Tenney was a tall lady with red hair and small blue framed glasses. Her favorite dress to wear was a white dress with black polka dots and bright red shoes. Carlie Rae loved Mrs. Tenney because her class was like a new adventure waiting to happen!

When Mama walked Carlie to her classroom, she gave her a kiss and hug then went to put her back pack in her cube and waited for the day to start. This was her first day; Carlie had a chance to meet all of her new classmates, which she found to be quite exciting!

Anya, was Carlie Rae's table mate. She had just turned 6 years old and wore her hair in two long French braids.

"Hi! My name is Anya! What's yours?" she said
in a booming voice.
"I'm Carlie Rae," Carlie said.
"Nice to meet you!" Anya said.

As the girls began to chatter about what their favorite ice cream was and the top color of the day, Mrs. Tenney entered the classroom. Mrs. Tenney had a wonderful way of showing off who she was. Carlie loved the polka dot dress she wore and her blue framed glasses.

"Good Moring class, as you all know my name is Mrs. Tenney and I will be your kindergarten teacher for the year, Welcome!"

"Hello Mrs. Tenney," the class said in unison.

"Hello to you all. Our first assignment will be to introduce something very important to you that begins with the same letter," said Mrs. Tenney. "Does everyone understand?"

Carlie could feel a sea of blue, green and brown eyes
beaming straight for Mrs. Tenney. She didn't know
what the word "describe" meant, so she was sure her
classmates did not.

"Mrs. Tenney, what does the word "describe" mean?"
Carlie said in a shy voice.

Sure, Carlie! The word DESCRIBE means to say out loud or write down what a person, place or thing may look like, how it feels, what it sounds like...

Carlie had to think of three words that began with the letter M and use them in a sentence.

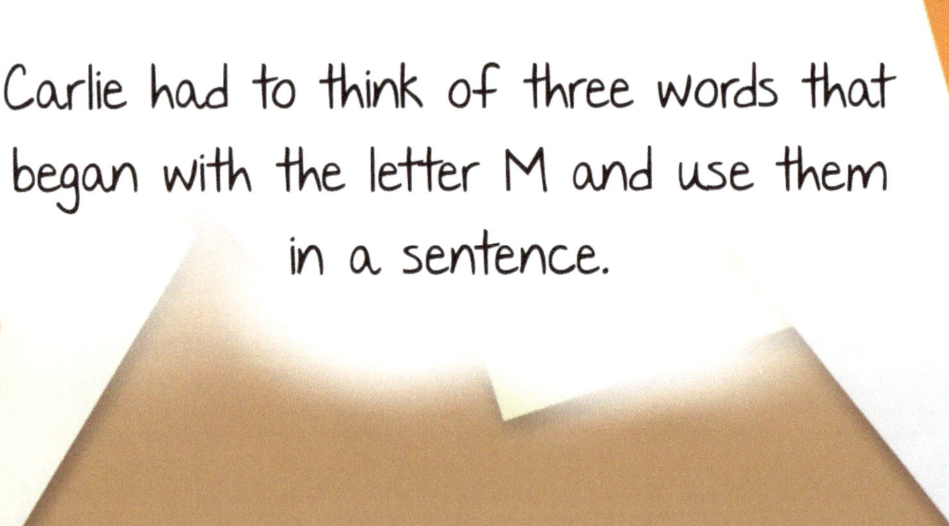

"Carlie thought. "Mama, Milk and Millie." Millie was Carlie's cat and often the one who went on brave adventures with her during her play time. Carlie could write those words because she practiced with Mama.

"Mama would you please give
Millie some milk?"

Carlie could tell that she would absolutely love Mrs. Tenney's class. All of her classmates were so much fun to be around.

With the day coming to a close, Carlie could
see her Mama through the window as she
arrived to pick her up.

As she walked to the car with her mother,
Carlie skipped and sang aloud:
Carlie Rae the adventurous one.
Carlie Rae is loads of fun!
Carlie Rae is the age of 6.
Carlie Rae loves magic tricks!

# About the Author

Letia Wyatt is a native of Hope, Arkansas who resides in Atlanta, Georgia. A graduate of the University of Central Arkansas who is currently in school for her Doctorate of Education in Organizational Leadership. When she is not in class you can catch her taking care of her plants, enjoying time with her friends, family, and sorority sisters. Her passion for poetry led her to write a children's book series and spread cheer with a little bit of sunshine.

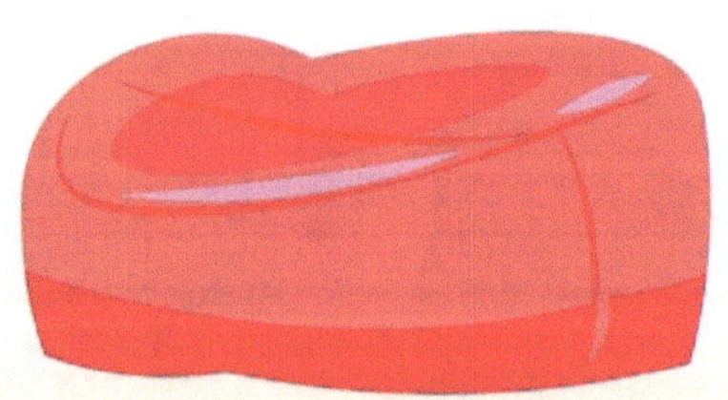